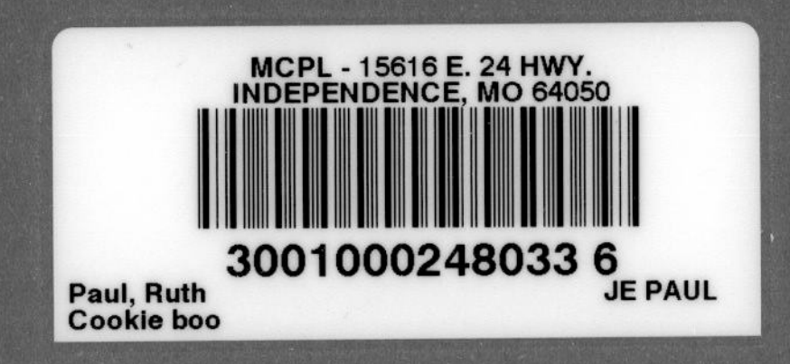
MCPL - 15616 E. 24 HWY.
INDEPENDENCE, MO 64050
3001000248033 6
Paul, Ruth
Cookie boo
JE PAUL

D1385063

WITHDRAW
from records of
Mid-Continent Public Library

Cookie
Boo
Ruth Paul
HARPER FESTIVAL
An Imprint of HarperCollinsPublishers

For Josie, Theo, and Penelope

— R.P.

HarperFestival is an imprint of HarperCollins Publishers

Copyright © 2020 by Ruth Paul
All rights reserved. Manufactured in China.
No part of this book may be used or reproduced in any manner whatsoever without written permission except in the case of brief quotations embodied in critical articles and reviews. For information address HarperCollins Children's Books, a division of HarperCollins Publishers, 195 Broadway, New York, NY 10007.

ISBN 978-0-06-286956-2

Typography by Honee Jang
20 21 22 23 24 SCP 10 9 8 7 6 5 4 3 2 1
❖
First Edition

Seven spooky cookies
sitting in a tin,
waiting for the moonlight
to let the magic in.

Trick or treat?
Lift the lid . . .
in the moonlight streams.

"BOO!" yell the cookies,

and Little Monster **screams!**

Out climb the cookies,
jumping to the floor.

"BOO!"
yell the cookies
to Doggy by the door.

Down through the garden,
out into the street.

"BOO!"

yell the cookies
to everything they meet.

"BOO!"

to the lamppost,

"BOO!"

to the car,

"BOO!"

to the fireflies flashing in a jar.

"BOO!" to the skeleton,

"BOO!"

to the ghost,

"BOO!"

to the witch's cat
sitting on a post.

Seven spooky cookies
playing on the slide.

Do they see the furry feet
poking out the side?

"BOO!" says Little Monster,
tricking all the treats.

"Yummy scrummy cookies!
Now you're mine to eat!"

Run spooky cookies,
scatter to and fro!

"BOO-HOO!"

cries Baby Bat.
"He's got me by the toe!"

Oh no!

Where to go?
Cookies, crisp with fright,
climb into a pumpkin
and huddle by the light.

Quiet, spooky cookies,
don't drop any crumbs.
Outside there's a monster . . .

Shhh . . .
Here he comes!
Hairy, scary Monster,
round the pumpkin creeps . . .

"BOO!"

yell the cookies,
and Little Monster leaps!

Scramble,
spooky cookies!

Flee with Baby Bat . . .

back past the happy ghost
howling with the cat.

Back past the skeleton
dancing all about,

back past the fireflies
(but let the critters out).

Back through the garden
to Doggy by the door.

Tiptoe quietly . . .
Listen to him snore!

Scale the walls!
Lift the lid!